A BIG BLUE TREE

글·그림 **미쓔**

미쓔 Missu

영국인 남편을 만나
천사 같은 두 아이와
행복한 일상을 살아가고 있는 아줌마!
그림을 좋아하는 마음 하나로
누구나 도전하면 '나만의 그림책'을
만들 수 있다는 것을 보여주고 싶다.
자신의 일상이 이 세상 가장 특별하고 유일한 이야기임을
깨닫고 많은 이들이 각자의 하루를 모아
마음속에 간직한 소중한 꿈을 이룰 수 있기를 바란다.

‖ 이메일 ajummaonfire@gmail.com
‖ 인스타 instagram.com/ajummaonfire

주인공 소개

우유(Milk)

작고 하얀 강아지.
성격은 까칠하지만
주인을 잘 따르며 애교가 많다.
망고의 관심을 반기지 않는다.

망고(Mango)

크고 순한 강아지.
노란 털에 근육질 몸매를 자랑한다.
우유를 좋아한다.
하지만 다른 개들이 다가오면
사냥개로 변신한다.

"
반가워,
제주도에 살고 있는 우유와 망고라고 해.
우리랑 같이 재미있게
영어그림책을 읽어보자고!
"

A big blue tree

Sight words

a, and, away, big, blue
can, come, down
find, for, funny, go
help, here, I, in, is, it
jump, little, look,
make, me, my, not, one
play, red, run, said, see
the, three, tree, to, two
up, we, where
yellow, you

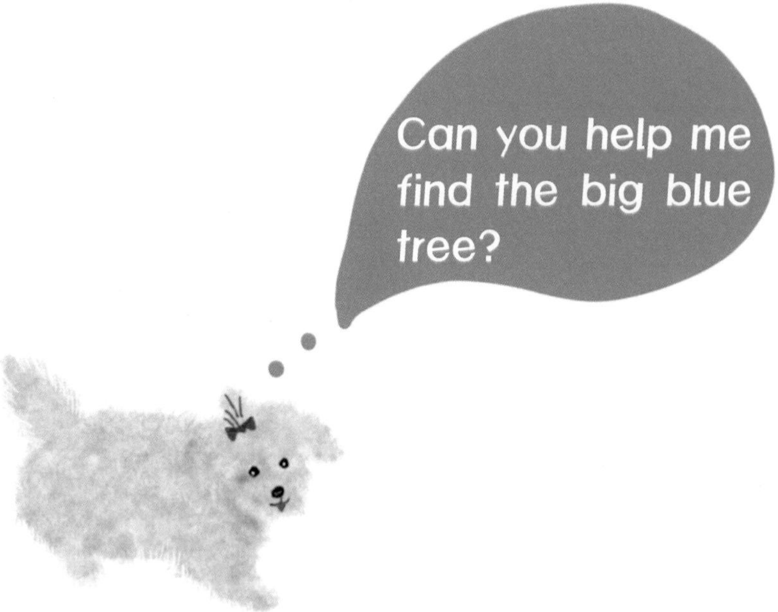
Can you help me find the big blue tree?

Can you find the big blue tree
for me?

A big blue tree?
Where can we see a big blue tree?

We go to look for it!

Here it is!

It is not a blue tree.
It is red.

Here it is!

It is not a blue tree.
It is yellow.

Here it is!
It is a blue tree.

It is not a big blue tree.
It is a little blue tree.

Where is it? Where is it?

I look up. I look down.

I see a tree.

It is big. It is blue.
It is a big blue tree.

I can see the big blue tree.
It is a funny tree.

I run away to the tree.

One, two and three, I jump up.
Look, it is me in a big blue tree.

Come down! Come down!
I said "Come down."

You come up.
We can play in the tree.

We can play in my big blue tree.

Come up here.
You can make it.

Funny cake

Sight words

all, am, are, a, ate, and, away
be, black, brown, but, big, blue
cake, cat, can, come, came
did, do, down, dog, eat, four
find, for, funny, get, good, go
have, he, help, here, I, in, into
is, it, jump, like, little, look
make, me, my, must, new, no
now, not, on, one, our, out
play, please, pretty, red, run
ran, ride, said, see, saw, say
she, so, soon, the, tree, three
to, two, that, there, they, this
too, up, under, we, where, want
was, well, went, what, white
who, will, with, you, yes, yellow

What is so funny?

A cat ate my pretty cake.

Well……
That is not funny at all.

It was!
A cat came and ate the cake.

A dog saw the cat.
The cat saw the dog.

The dog came to get the cat.

The cat ran into the cake.
The dog went into the cake too.

The cat ran out.
The dog ran out.

Cake was on the cat.
Cake was on the dog.
They did look funny with cake
on them.

But now I have no cake.
There is no cake to eat.

Who can help me make a new cake? Do you like cake?

Yes, I do!

Can you help me make a cake?

What cake do you want to make?

want to make a white cake but
t must be black and brown too.

Four, three, two, one······.

We make a cake.

The cake will be out soon.

We will eat the cake.
We will eat the cake under the tree!

Come here dog.
Come here cat.

We are under the tree.
We all eat the cake.
This is a good cake.
Our cake is good.

The dog and the cat play.

No cat! No!
Do not ride the dog!

They run. They run and run.
They run into the cake.

Now I am under the cake.
He is under the cake.
She is under the cake.
We are all under the cake.
We look funny under the cake.

But now······

I have no cake.
There is no cake to eat.

A BIG BLUE TREE

ⓒ미쓔 2024

발행 2024년 01월 10일

지은이 미쓔
펴낸이 한건희
펴낸곳 (주)부크크
출판등록 2014년 7월 15일(제2014-16호)
주소 서울특별시 금천구 가산디지털1로 119 SK트윈타워 A동 305호
전화 1670-8316
이메일 info@bookk.co.kr

ISBN 979-11-410-6613-0

www.bookk.co.kr